EARLY BIRD STORIES™

Police Officers
in My Community

Gina Bellisario Illustrated by **Cale Atkinson**

LERNER PUBLICATIONS ◆ MINNEAPOLIS

NOTE TO EDUCATORS

Find text recall questions at the end of each chapter. Critical-thinking and text feature questions are available on page 23. These help young readers learn to think critically about the topic by using the text, text features, and illustrations.

Copyright © 2019 by Lerner Publishing Group, Inc.

All rights reserved. International copyright secured. No part of this book may be reproduced, stored in a retrieval system, or transmitted in any form or by any means—electronic, mechanical, photocopying, recording, or otherwise—without the prior written permission of Lerner Publishing Group, Inc., except for the inclusion of brief quotations in an acknowledged review.

Lerner Publications Company
A division of Lerner Publishing Group, Inc.
241 First Avenue North
Minneapolis, MN 55401 USA

For reading levels and more information, look up this title at www.lernerbooks.com.

Photos on page 22 used with permission of: Maciej Bledowski/Shutterstock .com (police car); Bart Sadowski/Shutterstock.com (police badge); ChiccoDodiFC/Shutterstock.com (dog).

Main body text set in Billy Infant 22/28.
Typeface provided by SparkyType.

Library of Congress Cataloging-in-Publication Data

Names: Bellisario, Gina, author. | Atkinson, Cale, illustrator.
Title: Police officers in my community /Gina Bellisario ; illustrated by Cale Atkinson.
Description: Minneapolis : Lerner Publications, [2018] | Series: Meet a community helper (Early bird stories) | Audience: Age: 5–8. | Audience: K to Grade 3. | Includes bibliographical references and index.
Identifiers: LCCN 2017049675 (print) | LCCN 2017051847 (ebook) | ISBN 9781541524149 (eb pdf) | ISBN 9781541520202 (lb : alk. paper) | ISBN 9781541527096 (pb : alk. paper)
Subjects: LCSH: Police—Juvenile literature. | Communities—Juvenile literature.
Classification: LCC HV7922 (ebook) | LCC HV7922 .B455 2018 (print) | DDC 363.2—dc23

LC record available at https://lccn.loc.gov/2017049675

Manufactured in the United States of America
1-44356-34602-4/4/2018

TABLE OF CONTENTS

CHAPTER 1

OFFICER GABBY'S ASSIGNMENT

Today our class will find out what police officers do. Officer Gabby works at our school.

"I keep our neighborhood safe," says Officer Gabby. "And our school!" says Madeline.

Officer Gabby is a school resource officer.

She stops cars at the crosswalk.

She warns us about strangers.

NEVER TAKE RIDES FROM STRANGERS

"How did you get your assignment?" asks Phoebe.

"From my police department," says Officer Gabby.
"But first, I got training as a patrol officer."

We're happy she did!

What does a school resource officer do?

CHAPTER 2

OFFICER KEN AND A K-9

Most officers wear special clothes and tools for their police uniform.

We hear, "10-51 at 1422 Pine Street." Officer Gabby's uniform is talking!

"What's that noise?" asks Beckett.

"My police radio," she says. "Officer Ken is sharing information. He's on patrol."

Officer Ken drives his police car around neighborhoods.

Some patrol officers use helicopters or motorcycles. Others work on horseback!

Officer Ken has a K-9 partner named Badge. K-9 partners are also called police dogs.

K-9 partners sniff out people and hidden objects.

What is another name for a K-9 partner?

CHAPTER 3

TEAM SAFETY

"Do officers have people partners?" asks Ben.

"Many do," says Officer Gabby. "We also work with officers in other cities, states, and countries."

By teaming up,
officers keep us safer.

Not all police officers work in neighborhoods. State police patrol highways. They keep roads safe.

FBI agents protect the country. They gather information about crimes. They help catch people who break the law.

Even we can help! We buckle our seat belts.

We stand up against bullying.

When there's an emergency, we dial 9-1-1.

Police officers keep our community safe!

Where else might police officers work besides schools and neighborhoods?

21

LEARN ABOUT COMMUNITY HELPERS

Police officers are part of a community. A community is a group of people who live or work in the same city, town, or neighborhood.

Officers start training at a police academy. They go to this school after they finish high school. They study the law there. They practice directing traffic and other skills.

Officers talk over a police radio. They use numbers. Some numbers are paired with 10. The pairs are instructions. "10-51" is "tow truck needed." "10-4" is "I hear you." Using numbers is a fast way of talking.

Police cars have technology tools. A radio sends messages. A camera records what officers see. There's even room for a computer. Officers look up cars' license plate numbers. They also type reports.

K-9 partners use a special tool. That tool is their nose! A dog's sense of smell is a thousand times stronger than a human's. Police dogs can follow a trail for miles.

THINK ABOUT COMMUNITY HELPERS:
CRITICAL-THINKING AND TEXT FEATURE QUESTIONS

Why do you think police officers might need to talk fast over their radios?

What else might police dogs be able to do that human police officers can't?

What does this book's table of contents tell you?

Where in this book can you look up the meanings of certain words?

LERNER

SOURCE™

Expand learning beyond the printed book. Download free, complementary educational resources for this book from our website, www.lerneresource.com.

GLOSSARY

assignment: a specific job that is given to somebody

crime: something that is against the law

emergency: a problem that needs attention fast

law: a rule made by the government

9-1-1: a phone number to call during emergencies

patrol: to move around an area to protect it or to keep watch on people

TO LEARN MORE

BOOKS

George, Lucy M. *Police Officer*. London: QEB, 2016. Read this story about how Officer Seth and Officer Thea help out at a festival in their town.

Parkes, Elle. *Hooray for Police Officers!* Minneapolis: Lerner Publications, 2017. Check out this book to learn more about how police officers help their community.

WEBSITE

McGruff the Crime Dog
http://www.mcgruff-safe-kids.com
Visit this website to learn about safety, bullying, and more with McGruff the crime dog.

INDEX